WRAPPED IN RED

MIKA JOLIE

A My Happy Chaos Publishing Novel

Wrapped in Red
Copyright © 2015 Mika Jolie
ISBN: 978-1519509710

Cover design by Dawné Dominique
Image by The Reed Files
Edited by PK Designs
Proofread by Colleen Snibson
All cover art and logo copyright © 2015 by Mika Jolie

PUBLISHER
My Happy Chaos Publishing
www.mikajolie.com

Dedication

To my husband, thank you so much for all of your support and for taking over our happy chaos when I need to write. A toast to our lifetime of dating. You are my biggest fan and that makes you even sexier than you already are. I love you! Aujourd'hui, Demain, Toujours.

My wonderful group of writers: WWLR and the ladies at Three Chicas and a Book. PK Designs, DusktilDawnDesigns and Colleen Snibson. What can I say? You ROCK!

A big awesome hooray to Bonnie Messinger, you continue to push me and make me better.

Last but not least, to all the readers—without you this wouldn't be as much fun. Thank you so much for all you've helped me to accomplish.

Anyone else I may have missed. Fear not, there are more books to come.

Love you all!!!

Chapter One

"Honey. Our baby's here."
Lou Lou Who—*How the Grinch*
Stole Christmas

Twelve days before Christmas

A piercing wail cut through the stillness of the night, drowning out the silence. Minka flinched. Heavy-lidded eyes popped open. Ears perked, she waited. Within seconds, another sharp bawl lit the baby monitor on her nightstand.

She flung the comforter to the side and sat on the edge of the bed. The December air clung to her body, turning her skin tight with goosebumps. Pressing her fists against her lids, she tried to rub the burn from her sleep-deprived eyes. Instead, a dull, pulsing agony shot straight to her skull. On her nightstand, she grabbed her phone for a quick time check. Four in the morning. Perfect. Only thirty minutes ago, she'd been up with Sebastian's older sister, Maya. The curse of twins, they were never on the same schedule.

In a zombie-like state, she scrambled to her feet and lumbered out of the room. As she did so, she peered at the long-limbed, masculine form. Jason remained motionless, paralyzed in sleep. He'd have to be dead or unconscious to not hear the twins shrieking at the top of their lungs.

A burning sensation zipped through her chest—acid build-up from that extra piece of cinnamon coffee cake she ate at Forrest's and Claire's. Not that she'd needed the additional slice. Hell, cake was never on the *need* list. However, coffee and cake meant double the deliciousness, and zonked out from the daily grind of motherhood while Jason had been on a business trip, she'd managed to convince herself cake had eggs. Eggs were healthy. Therefore cake fell somewhere between good and evil.

Her chest retaliated and zinged once more. Acid reflux, sleep deprivation, and maybe twenty pounds over her pre-pregnancy weight meant she was back in double-digit sized jeans. Just in time for Christmas.

Yippee! If only she had a scale.

Scale. Ha! Bad, bad idea. She'd been down that path. She was once addicted to the thing, and had even stuffed the metallic equipment in her luggage on her first trip to Martha's Vineyard. It had taken some work—almost losing Jason actually—but she got the memo: *love your body and stop giving a damn what the scale says.*

Definitely not gonna go down that road again. The new-and-improved Minka Greene Montgomery was strong, confident, and at ease in her skin. Each time a worrying thought emerged, she should be wise enough to mentally jot it down on a notepad, wrap it around a stone, and throw it into the bottom of the ocean.

Except lately, an eerie fog, gray and ominous, slogged through her.

Another piercing cry, similar to a wounded animal, snapped her from her *poor Minka* moment. This time, Sebastian sounded impatient. At nine weeks old, the twins sleep pattern was still unpredictable—two to four hours at a time—day or night. The result—lots of sleep for them, a very irregular and tiring schedule for mommy. She fed. She comforted. She changed diapers, lots of them.

When she wasn't doing that, there was the breast-pumping situation, a total mood killer. The day Jason barged in on her—with two suction cups connected to her nipples while being milked like a cow—had been mortifying.

Ahhh! The joys of motherhood.

She hurried down the hall and pushed the door open. Bas seemed to have sensed her presence the minute she stepped into the room and greeted her with a soft cooing sound instead of the shrieking cry.

"Charming little bugger. Just like your daddy." She reached into the crib and scooped Bas' warm body to her chest. Chubby bracelets of fat at his wrists and ankles rubbed against her arm. His sweet smell, fresh and innocent, almost made her forget the sharp pain from the horizontal incision on her bikini line. Recovery from the C-section, which happened a little over two months ago, was still hell. Her abs had been cut in half, making it impossible to do a sit-up without pain, which meant goodbye to ripped abs.

A low chuckle spilled past her lips. She'd never had rock-hard abs—or been a fan of sit-ups—but it'd been a lofty goal. Keely and the others seemed to enjoy planks. Maybe she'd give those a try. One day.

She stepped on the area rug, wriggled her toes into its warmth, then lowered herself into the rocking chair. Gently, she brushed aside the top of her nightgown and cradled Bas to her chest, offering him her nipple. Her son shifted his head, which, in baby language, meant he just wanted to be held.

"Your sister woke up half an hour ago," she said in a low voice, stuffing her breast back in its package, then softly rocking Bas back to sleep. "Why can't you guys get on the same schedule?" In response, baby Bas let out another one of his delightful mews, melting her heart.

About an hour later, Minka flopped back in bed. If she played her cards right, she could get forty-five minutes of sweet, wonderful sleep. Next to her, Jason's big body stirred.

"Come here," he said, his voice low and rough with sleep.

Her stomach coiled into a tight knot, but she did as he bid. One arm circled her waist as he pulled her against his hard-muscled chest.

"Who woke up?" he mumbled against her ear.

"Sebastian." She nestled into his warmth, welcoming him home. His travels had increased right about the time she gave birth—some overseas, some in other states. He'd been gone more often than he'd been home, which meant it'd just been her and the twins.

In the past, she'd rationalized that his travels came with running Montgomery Corporation with his father. Since the babies arrived, she ached for him to be home more frequently, like every day.

"Maya slept through the night," her husband noted, as if that ever happened.

She wanted to laugh at his remark, but since her energy gauge had fallen past empty, she said, "Nowhere near."

"We don't have a tree." His voice echoed in the vast darkness around them.

"A tree?"

"A Christmas tree." After a slight pause, he added, "Christmas is twelve days away."

She said nothing. Other than the crackling sound coming from the baby monitors, all noises were muted.

"Our favorite time of year," Jason continued, a slight edge to his words.

She understood the tension in his voice. They didn't even have a wreath on the front door, never mind a Christmas tree, or a decorated house.

"We don't need to get a tree." She had been on mommy mode. Former exciting leisure activities, Christmas included, had since given way to compelling interests in baby matters—the quality of a breastfeeding, the magnitude of a burp, or the color of a bowel movement.

"Why is that?"

How could she vocalize that the duties of motherhood had sapped the pleasure from what used to be a joyous time in her life. If she had to choose between sleep or decking the halls, and everything else that came with Christmas—cooking, cleaning, wrapping, shopping—she would choose sleep without any hesitation. Not that she was a Grinch, just overwhelmed.

"Well." A nervous chuckle escaped her throat. Physically depleted at the end of most days, harvesting a tree at Herring Creek Farm, much less decorating one, was no longer a priority. Her heart was too dark. With both of them running in opposite directions, this season failed to capture the magic of their first Christmas together. "I'm sure all the trees are gone. As you said, Christmas is only twelve days away."

"We're getting a tree," he said in a cool, but determined tone. "I don't care if it's the Charlie Brown Christmas tree. The more traditions we can build into Maya's and Bas' life, the better."

She nodded. No point arguing. The invisible wound around her heart continued its silent bleeding. Jason's palm traced her stomach, teasing her in a slow circle around her navel. Only a man could sleep through two crying babies, then be fully alert and ready for sex five minutes later.

"I've missed you." His lips grazed against her neck—a gesture that normally sent her head spinning, and always managed to get that spot between her thighs throbbing with need. Tonight, while her body failed to scream the usual *take me Jason anthem*, it did manage to stir a bit. That is, until his palm moved south and brushed the tough, heaped-up scar on her lower abdomen. The familiar disquietude she had been struggling with reared its ugly head.

She didn't want to be touched.

Minka tensed. Her hand moved to her bikini line, as if protecting the scar tissue from the contact.

"What's wrong?" he asked

"Nothing," she responded quickly, too quickly. "I'm tired."

"Not ready?"

She wanted to have sex.

Kind of.

Not really.

With a baby at her breast most of the day, any additional physical connection was one more demand on her body. Truth was, she had no desire for sex. Her one little secret she wasn't ready to share with anyone—not with her twin Keely, her friend Claire, or even her BFF Lily. They would think she'd lost her mind. All of them were rolling in some sort of bliss—happily married, newly engaged, new baby.

Nope. She couldn't disclose this little secret to any member of her tight-knit circle.

Never. Ever.

She'd have to drown in her sorrows all by herself, thank you, very much. Two months after giving birth to the twins, she should be back and ready to go—physically, mentally, and emotionally. But damn it, she was tired. All. The. Fucking. Time.

"I'm sorry," she said in a low voice, so low she wasn't sure Jason heard her. "It's just…" What exactly was she going to say? The disproportionate burden of caring for the twins had diminished her libido?

That would make her a failure. As the mother, she was supposed to be the base of their family—balanced, a multi-tasker, always primped up. Her mother had done it. Really well too.

The fear of failing—lodged deep inside her—stirred. Tears burned behind her eyes and threatened to spill. Not the 'I'm glad you're home' tears, either. These leaned more toward sad. The joy she thought she would experience once the twins were born had somehow managed to slip from her hands before she had an opportunity to savor the moment.

She should be happy. Her life was perfect—a handsome husband who adored her, healthy twin babies, great friends, family, and she was adjusting to motherhood. But lately, life had taken a very difficult course. She'd become a walking zombie, dead on the inside, but functioning by all outside appearances.

Jason rolled onto his back, his arms still around her, holding her tight against him. "Guess what?"

"What?" she repeated, eyes closed, head resting on his chest.

"You didn't tell me you love me."

Of course she'd told him. Definitely when he'd first come home—the three little words were deeply embedded as part of their normal every day greeting. She replayed the scene from earlier in her head—the kissing, the smiles, the hugs. A vise closed around her heart. Guilt—the ugly scar sat proudly, not on her stomach, but in her brain.

"I do...love you." The words stumbled from her mouth.

Chapter Two

"One thing about trains: It doesn't matter where they're goin'. What matters is deciding to get on."
The Conductor—*The Polar Express*

Eleven days before Christmas

No way in hell was she going to get the jeans past her thighs, stretchy material or not. Minka squeezed her lower lip between her teeth, shifted her hips to the left, right, and pulled.

The denims moved above her knees and stopped. Okay, progress, however small. She inhaled, sucked in her stomach as much as possible and tugged hard. This time the cotton fabric cooperated and slid over her ass.

Self-high-five!

Almost there.

Now to zip. No problem there. Yes!

Today was her day. Jason had taken over watching the twins, which gave her kid-free, quality time with Lily.

Okay, pull really, really tight, get the button into that tiny little hole and voilà!

Easy as pie. Never mind, she wasn't good at baking pies.

She took in another breath.

Her waist whispered, *not so fast*.

Stubborn little fuck.

"Everything alright in there?" Lily asked from outside the fitting room.

Surrendering to the power of leftover pregnancy weight, Minka gave up on the button. "I'm fine. Just need a second or two."

Or a couple of months of pure exercise torture. Why couldn't she be an athlete like Lily or take up jogging like her husband?

Oh wait, she'd tried that once. As if running weren't challenging enough, her boobs had thumped against her chest the whole freakin' time, threatening to give her black eyes. Talk about a full-contact sport. No thanks. In life, there were a few things she could live without—graphic breasts bouncing and back pain—ranked pretty high on the list.

"*Chérie*," Gerard, the co-owner of *La Jolie* called in his deep French accent. "We can get you another pair that is...um...more fitting."

Translation: Accept your fatness and bask in its ambiance.

"These are fine. Thanks," she responded, forcing her voice to sound more upbeat than she felt.

Okay, she lied. See, she had this grand idea that after giving birth, the weight would magically fall off. Well, that had been her goal. Yet, here she was, the twins were nine weeks on the dot, and the fat was jiggling in all the same places as before.

Mission failed. Actually, more like a complete disaster.

On top of that, Christmas was eleven days away. Hell for her. She'd been eating since Thanksgiving. The holidays were another guaranteed ten pounds. All she had to do was inhale the sweet aroma of one of Adam's homemade *Panettone*, and she'd gained five pounds.

Just her luck, attractive men who took significant pride in feeding their women and getting them fat in the process surrounded her.

Well, she was alone in this struggle. Lily had sneezed and lost all of her pregnancy weight. Claire and Keely were still blessed with the pre-baby, toned-and-tight bodies. She glanced at her reflection in the mirror—thick frizzy dark brown hair framed her face, sunken eyes stared back at her.

Her hands fell to her side in defeat as she dropped limply into the shabby armchair in the fitting room. This was her day to have fun, relax. Yet, here she was, bottomless, sad at the horizons of her mind, where she'd kept everything clouded. A hard, painful lump pressed in the back of her throat as the tears began to form, and her last shred of normalcy shattered into a million pieces.

From her mouth came a raw cry. Between a little chuckle and a half sigh, she buried her face in her hands and gave way to the enormity of her grief.

She sobbed.

Emotional pain dripped between her fingers, raining down her arms.

"Minka." Lily hugged Minka's shaking shoulders. "Hon, what's going on?"

"*Est-elle malade? Enceinte?*" The French shop owner barged into the tight dressing room in a heavy-knit Christmas sweater.

Minka choked a laugh through her tears. No, she wasn't sick or pregnant, just down in the blues and overweight. For fuck's sake, she wanted those fucking jeans to fit.

"Should we call Doctor Desvareaux?" Gerard continued.

Oh God, the last thing she wanted was Forrest to find her crying with her pants undone. He'd go straight to his brother and tell him everything.

Wiping her face, she flashed Gerard a polite smile. "I'm sorry."

"Give us a minute, Gerard." Lily slipped a hand through the boutique owner's arm and tried to shoo him away.

"Apology not necessary." Gerard stood firm, resisting Lily's silent request. "You are one of our favorite customers. Louise is preparing tea for you both. Join us when you're ready." His gaze swept over Minka's face for a beat, concern filled his eyes. Then, with a slight nod, he exited the fitting room.

"I have to make a quick stop at Vapor," Lily said once they were alone. "Come meet me there."

"I should go home."

"No. This is girlfriends' day, remember? We must do lunch."

Half an hour later, Minka ambled through the bustling streets of downtown Edgartown to meet Lily at Vapor. Around her, people swarmed like bees in and out of the crowded coffee shops and bakeries. Shop windows were decorated with wreaths, Santa Claus, garlands, ornaments, and lights. The aroma of hot-roasted chestnuts wafted through the town. Martha's Vineyard was a perfect Christmas postcard.

She crossed the street and entered Vapor. *Happy Christmas (War is Over)* by John Lennon echoed throughout the room, evoking memories of her and Jason humming to the tune. She sniffed back another round of tears, waved to Adam, and headed to Lily's table.

"I ordered your fave." Lily motioned toward the plate on the table, a proud smile on her face.

"Thanks." Minka sat and focused on the Italian sausage and tortellini soup, one of Vapor's greatest creations. The broth smelled delicious and comforting. Not diet food at all, but just what the doctor ordered.

"You, my friend, have postpartum depression." Lily reached over and squeezed her hand. "We need to get you counseling."

Pursing her lips in contemplation, Minka tucked a wayward curl behind her hear. Postpartum depression. Nope. Not her. She'd bonded with the twins. Sure, at times, she felt overwhelmed. Not like, 'hey, this new mommy thing is hard,' but more like 'I can't do this, and I'm never going to be able to do this.' In fact, on several occasions, she found herself wondering whether she should have become a mother in the first place.

That didn't mean she had postpartum depression. It had to be fatigue. She was tired as hell, but that happened with newborns. If she could get the twins on the same schedule, everything would get better.

She looked around the usual Vapor crowd. Adam was at the bar talking to Maxi. He'd agreed to cover for Jason at the last minute so that she could meet up with Lily.

"How are you sleeping?"

Minka lowered her gaze to the menu on the table. Although Lily's voice was casual, she knew her friend well enough to see this was a loaded question and the beginning of an interrogation.

"Fine," she answered in a voice she hoped matched Lily's tone. Truth was, sleep had become a fleeting chore, eluding her at a time when rest was all she needed to refuel. Most nights, she found herself wrestling in the dark, consumed by thoughts tumbling through her mind in rapid succession. Problems she had already solved reemerged for another examination. Things she mustn't forget for the next day nagged at her brain.

Monsters didn't always sleep under the bed. Lately they'd taken a permanent space inside her head.

"You're lying."

She dragged her gaze from the table and met Lily's probing eyes. "I don't have postpartum depression."

Lily raised a brow.

Minka blew a handful of curls away from her face. "I passed the test." She had examined each question and answered in a way so that she would appear fine and happy. Deep down, she had wanted to cry, to run away, or maybe stay pregnant a little longer.

"That screening done at the hospital before discharge, while I'm glad it's there, is pure bullshit." Lily leaned back in the chair and fixed her with a stare. "You and I know how to answer those questions and pretend all is fine."

Minka bit a chunk of her cheek inside of her mouth. Her phone dinged, indicating an incoming text. Grateful for the interruption, she swiped the screen, and a picture of the twins, in Christmas outfits her husband must have purchased, appeared with a message from Jason.

Bonding with these angels. We love you, Mommy.

She traced her finger over the image. Sets of blue and hazel eyes stared at her, and rosebud lips were spread into smiles. Something quivered low in her belly, but just as quickly, the darkness she'd been struggling with grew steadily until it dominated her emotions.

She slid the phone across the table. "Jason sent a picture of the twins."

Lily looked down at the screen. When her gaze returned to Minka, her features softened into a warm smile. "Babies are so adorable, aren't they?"

"Yes they are." She stuffed the phone in her purse.

"How's married life?"

"Fine."

"It's been nine weeks you got the green light?" Lily asked casually.

"For?"

"Sex with your husband."

"What?" Minka tucked a few stray curls behind her ear.

"You know," Lily continued, playfully pushing the subject. "You both get naked, touch, kiss, and a whole lotta sucking, blowing—"

"You can stop," she interrupted and shot her friend the *not now* look. "I know what sex is."

"But you have no desire to go there, do you?" Lily had a way of not mincing her words, one of the qualities Minka admired in her friend, even when she found herself the target.

"It's not what you think." There was an odd tightness in her voice, and seeing the way Lily arched a brow, Minka knew she had revealed a corner of her own thoughts. She shifted in her seat and fixed her gaze on the plate in front of her.

"You're in love with your husband." Lily reached over and gently squeezed her hand, drawing Minka's attention back to her. "And he loves you so damn much. Talk to him. Tell him the truth."

"I don't have—"

"Yeah, you do," Lily interjected. "That's not something to be ashamed of. Between ten and twenty percent of new mothers experience some kind of PPD."

"How do you know that?" Had she been so consumed with her pregnancy that she'd failed to notice anything different with Lily after she gave birth?

"Paige told me."

Paige was a nurse, close friends with the Serrano brothers, and Lily's informant on all things medical.

Still, the idea of not being there for the woman she viewed as a sister didn't sit well. "I'm sorry. I didn't realize you were going through a hard time after giving birth to Christina."

"I struggled here and there. I had a light case of baby blues and needed to adjust." Lily leaned forward, a perplexed expression on her face. "But honey, I contacted Paige because I've been concerned about you."

"You told Paige I have postpartum?"

"No. I called her and asked a question. Minka, postpartum is not something to be ashamed of."

Baby blues were normal. Nothing but hormonal changes, PMS on steroids. Postpartum depression though...not her.

"Easy to say when the problem is not your own."

"Ouch." Lily grimaced.

Minka took a shaky breath, peered at Lily and caught a hint of hurt in her friend's eyes. "God, I'm sorry. That was harsh and not deserved," she apologized, wishing she could take back the snarky remark. "I'm just tired. You think I'm crazy."

"Sleep deprivation makes us all a bitch. But since I have all this love for you *chica*, you get a free pass."

"Still, I'm sorry," she apologized again. No point denying the daggers in her words.

"It's okay. I had bouts here and there where everything annoyed me, including my sexy husband."

Minka smiled in spite of herself. She was all too familiar with that feeling. "What did you do?"

"I had a few sessions with Adam's counselor." She shrugged. "It helped. I can give you her information."

She didn't need it, but neither was she in any mood to argue. "Sure, I'll take it." Just in case.

Chapter Three

"Forgive me, Mr. Claus. I'm afraid I've made a
terrible mess of your holiday."
Jack Skellington—*The Nightmare*
before Christmas

Ten days before Christmas

The Christmas tree stood tall—brightly illuminated with big, traditional, multi-colored dome lights. Incandescent glow from red, blue, green, yellow, and gold sparkled against exquisite ornaments. Kelly Clarkson's *Winter Dreams* played softly in the room, telling Minka how joyous she should be.

She wasn't.

If anything, the whole atmosphere was another reminder that the magic of Christmas was out of reach.

Two hours into the traditional party at Martha's Way, Minka watched as people strolled in and out of the bustling room. The merry dining hall screamed happiness. Warm smiles on familiar faces as they sipped champagne or hot drinks topped with generous layers of whipped cream. Moments of loud, spirited laughter erupted on occasion over continuous chatter. The mood at Martha's Way was festive, no doubt about that. As always, Jason had put together another flawless event.

Her gaze followed her husband as he weaved through the crowd—broad powerful shoulders, inviting blue eyes, days-old scruff covering his chin, and a vibe that screamed full-tilt danger. As he walked, he ran his fingers through the tapered edges of his blond hair. The slight movement made his well-worked biceps bunch under the sleeve of his three-piece black suit, and her stomach did that familiar little flip that only Jason could garner. He was easy on the eyes, exuded sexuality and confidence from every pore. A year into their marriage and with each passing day, her love for him had gotten deeper, more complete, more bewitching.

Watching him took her back to the first time she saw him, the night of Keely and Blake's engagement party here at the inn. He'd been beautiful then and was even more so now. To think, two years later, here they were, married with twins.

Speaking of the twins, she dug inside her purse for her phone. No message from Forrest or Claire. They had volunteered to watch Maya and Bas for the night, an act of kindness that allowed her to attend the traditional pre-Christmas dinner Jason threw for his staff. On top of that, she even felt pretty in the black swing dress that had been tucked away in her closet. Her last *I-feel-good* purchase before the twins. She eyed her phone again.

No news meant good news, right?

What could possibly go wrong in the course of a few hours? Forrest was probably the most responsible of the group. More importantly, not only was he the twins' uncle, godfather, and Jason's brother, he was a doctor for Pete's sake. Besides, if something had happened to one of the twins, they would have been notified.

Still, better to be safe than sorry. Her fingers moved swiftly as she sent a quick text to her friends.

How are things going?

One second passed. Two seconds. Three seconds. She eyed the screen. No response. Minka shifted uncomfortably. Her heart rate accelerated as her mind spun with a carousel of ideas, each more worrisome than the last.

What if the twins were hungry?

They might need their diapers changed. Dirty diapers resulted in bad, painful rashes.

She was the only one well versed with the twins' emotions and habits. A little over two months old, their speech pattern consisted of crying, gurgles, oohs and aahs.

Forrest and Claire were still in rekindled romantic bliss and planning a wedding, always touching, kissing, totally lost and oblivious to anything around them. They probably weren't paying any attention to Maya and Sebastian, which meant they weren't as attentive to the twins as they should be. Guilt ate and pestered her. She should have listened to her gut and stayed home, let Jason attend this party by himself. The twins needed her much, much more.

The fireplace crackled. With brows drawn together, she studied her telephone screen. Nothing from her friends. A sudden surge of fear came without warning. Her heart banged against her chest wall, loud and irregular, but she barely heard it. The twins consumed her every thought.

Minka cleared the burn in her throat and peeled away from the corner window. The heels of her shoes tap-tapped on the hardwood floor as she weaved through the crowd toward her husband. One step. Two steps. Three steps.

She came to an abrupt stop. Her eyes narrowed on Jason and the pretty woman whose head tilted forward in the inviting way that said she wanted a man. To make matters worse, he leaned into her and placed a kiss on each side of Lisa's face. The Chief Editor of the *Massachusetts Gazette* flicked her blonde hair, laughed, and held on to his arms.

Minka's stomach churned with a mixture of jealousy and anger. Blood rushed in her ears and her pulse skyrocketed. Logic skittered through her mind and tried to point out that kissing on the cheeks was a common European greeting. Technically, her husband was half-French from his late Mother's side. He was even fluent in the language of love.

Whatever! Born in America, raised in America, that made him as every bit American as she was. Besides, Lisa had wanted him from day one.

What the hell?

She wasn't jealous or threatened by the other woman. She couldn't be.

Minka sucked in a breath. Not wanting to give the green-eyed monster any more leeway, she lowered her gaze to her wedding band for a beat. Jason loved her unconditionally. And she loved him. She looked up just in time to catch Caribbean-Sea-blue orbs watching her, a smile on Jason's handsome face as he continued talking to Lisa. Across the room, he signaled for her to join them.

Jealous or not, none of that mattered. The most important thing now was to make sure their children were fine and safe. She plodded toward her husband and the beautiful, inviting Lisa. Her heartbeat echoed in the hall.

Ba dum. Ba dum. Ba dum.

"Lisa, remember my wife, Minka?" Jason pulled her into him.

"Of course. Congratulations on the twins," Lisa said in a tone that actually appeared genuine. "Jason was gushing over them and you."

"Thank you." She smiled at Lisa, in a way she hoped came across as warm and friendly, before turning to Jason. "We should leave."

"What?" he asked in a confused voice.

"Claire and Forrest aren't responding."

"To?" Worry creased his forehead.

The scent of the pine needles grew heavy. She let out a frustrated breath. "To my text."

"I'll see you around, Jay. Good to see you, Minka, and congrats again," Lisa said before walking away, leaving her alone with Jason.

With a slight tug, he pulled them a few steps away from everyone. "What's going on, Minka?"

"They're not responding to my text."

"And…"

"Something could be wrong. I feel something is wrong. If you don't want to come with me, I'll go."

He glanced at his watch, exasperation etched on his handsome face. "Give me a second to speak to Nora."

Before she could answer, he released her arm and walked away. She watched him engaged in a brief conversation with Nora, the woman who managed Martha's Way. After a few nods and smiles, the two hugged. Then he was back by her side.

"I'm sorry, Jason, but…" she started, needing to apologize, or at least try to get him to understand why she was anxious to get home.

"Let's go." Jason palm rested in the center of her back, no sign of intimacy in his touch.

Chapter Four

*"I never thought it was such a bad little tree. It's not
bad at all, really. Maybe it just needs a little love."*
Linus—*Charlie Brown Christmas*

Forty minutes later, the black Jeep snaked along the
paved roads of Katama. Other than the efficient
purr of the well-oiled engine, a strained hush cloaked
the space between them, a clear indication of built-up
tension. In the corner of her eye, she caught a glimpse
of his profile. His jaw was stretched tight. One hand
gripped the steering, while the other shifted gears.
She'd always admired the subtle tilt of his head when
he turned onto the road, as if every movement seemed
planned ahead of time.

Observing his movements, a sigh escaped her lips.
She wanted to touch him and run her fingers through
his hair. However, the chill between them crisped her
skin. She rubbed her hands together and forced them
into submission.

Less than two years together, they were technically still in the learning phase. Nonetheless, she knew
her husband well enough to tell when he was ticked
off. Right now was a perfect example.

Her hands twitched and she could feel a vein pulsing in her forehead. Turning her face to the window, she put her fist under her chin and focused her attention on the winter's night—a dull, starless sky scowled down at her with impending doom. She dug deep, stayed poised, and didn't spring into action until the rhythmic clatter of tires slid to a stop.

She located the clip of her seat belt well before the Jeep's engine groaned and shut down. Swiftly, she grabbed the door handle, pushed it open, and charged inside the noiseless house. Without a backward glance at Jason, she sprinted up the stairs to Maya's bedroom, then Sebastian's. No sign of the twins anywhere.

"Jason!" she called to her husband as she rushed down the stairs. Her heart thundered in her chest as her brain ran amok with dread and dark thoughts.

"Shh." His index finger pressed against his lips. "Come with me."

Taking her hand in his, he led her down the hall into the dimly lit family room. On the grand, Chesterfield, cocoa-leather sofa, Forrest slouched low, with his head lying back on the cushion, and his signature black framed glasses slightly crooked upon his nose. Maya lay securely tucked on his chest. Not too far away, Claire—Forrest's fiancée—was in the same position. Her ebony hair trussed up in a bun, with a few loose strands brushing her shoulders. Her arms circled around baby Bas as he nuzzled against her. All four of them were fast asleep.

Minka let out a deep breath of relief, her heart slowly steadying. Jason gave her hand a squeeze, then walked over to his brother and lightly nudged his shoulder.

"You're home early," Forrest said as he carefully came to his feet. With one hand protectively on Maya's back, he lowered his head and centered his glasses on his nose with his forefinger. At the sound of his voice, Claire slowly opened her eyes and rose to her feet.

"Yeah. Minka was a little worried," Jason informed the others.

In other words, Minka went fucking crazy. She tried to plaster a smile across her face and failed.

"Oh." Claire's chestnut eyes ping-ponged from Jason to Minka. "Did we accidentally butt dial you when the twins were crying?"

"There was a moment of chaos," Forrest admitted with a chuckle. "But we huddled and got a firm grip on the situation." His gray eyes locked with Claire's. The two seemed to share a *one day it will be us* moment and a confidence that said they'd be ready.

Minka's heart rattled. Failure squeezed her throat.

"See *chèrie*," Jason said, snapping her from the dark place she seemed to love visiting lately. "They had everything under control." His voice revealed none of the frustration she knew was roiling below the surface.

Ignoring her husband's steely gaze, she walked past him to Forrest. "You guys weren't answering your messages." She extended her hands to relieve her brother-in-law of Maya, still snuggling comfortably against his chest. "I can take her."

"We'll put them to bed," Claire volunteered. She smiled at Forrest, her face glowing with delight. "Be right back."

Once alone with Jason, the odd, uncomfortable hush returned. Minka watched, waiting for the storm to come. Jason removed his jacket and threw it on the sofa, then quietly started tidying up the room.

"Jason."

"Not now, Minka," he interjected, his voice tight and controlled.

Minka pursed her lips. They were good at reading each other's moods, and right now Jason's screamed *pissed off*. The unstable part of her begged to press on and make him comprehend her rationality, but logic told her she understood his frustration. In quiet silence, she picked up a few pillows from the floor and placed them back where they belonged.

"Sorry. We were going to clean up," Claire said, walking back into the room with her fiancé.

Jason waved a dismissing hand at Claire. "Don't worry about it. We appreciate you watching the twins for the night."

"Anytime, little brother," Forrest said with a teasing glint in his voice, no sign of the anger he'd harbored for months after discovering one of his closest friends was actually his brother.

"Yeah, we had fun." Claire let out one of her little laughs as Forrest pulled her to him.

Minka's stomach fluttered. Longing clawed deep inside, but she clamped it back down. She couldn't remember the last time she and Jason were that affectionate, just a man and a woman, husband and wife, lovers, cuddling, touching.

"Forrest is officially convinced he wants five children," Claire continued.

"Definitely more than two," Forrest confirmed.

Jason laughed. "I think the three of us suffer from only child syndrome."

Minka folded the red throw and placed it on the chaise.

"Technically, you and I don't fall in the only child category," Forrest reminded his brother. They might have different mothers but they shared Charles Montgomery as their father.

"Very true," Jason agreed.

"Still hosting Christmas Eve dinner?" Forrest asked.

Now that they were all either married or soon to be tying the knot, the Wolf Pack had established a new tradition for the holidays. One couple would host Christmas Eve dinner each year. Since luck had been on her side, she and Jason won the coin toss and were first at bat. There was only one problem. Ten days before Christmas, she had no urge to have her house filled with friends and family.

"Yeah, why do you ask?" Jason answered.

Claire examined the empty spot by the window where the tree stood last Christmas. "Not decorating this year?"

Minka brushed a handful of curls away from her face, a smile staining her lips. Her eyes stayed on the unoccupied space where she and Jason had put their first Christmas tree.

Memories of last Christmas slashed through her—the happiness that soaked into her bones as they stood back, hand in hand, looking at the blinking lights wrapped around the tree. The sound of Andrea

Bocelli and Mary J Blige singing *What Child is This.* The smell of roasted chestnuts mixed with the smoky scent of from the fireplace had been intoxicating.

Her heart pinched with sadness. She loved Christmas, but could now admit that the Grinch had taken control. If it'd help, she'd gladly send out a plea: *Christmas Magic missing. If found, please return.*

Jason ran his hand over his face, something he always did when stressed. "We haven't picked one up yet," he said in a deceptively calm voice.

Minka bit her lip, not saying anything. She'd been so focused on the twins, and, until two days ago, Jason had been away. The moment never presented itself, unlike last year when they'd made everything about Christmas a priority. Their favorite holiday went from meaning everything to nothing in such a short span of time.

An uncomfortable silence loomed for a moment until Forrest spoke. "Lily's brothers sent a group message. They'll be here for Christmas."

"Yeah, they challenged us to a basketball game on the day before Christmas Eve." Jason chuckled. Tension continued playing over his handsome features. "They're outnumbered. Four of us to three of them."

"I asked Tyler to step in for them," Forrest informed his brother.

Jason's brows went up. "Tyler can't play for shit."

"So not fair," Claire pointed out without a hint of regret.

The two men laughed, obviously pleased with their genius plotting.

"We'll kick their asses," Forrest noted, "go home, shower, and head over here."

His brother nodded. "Sounds like a plan."

The brothers shook hands, which transitioned into a hug-like, semi-embrace, lasting no more than one second, and finished with a firm slap on the back, solidifying their manhood.

Forrest grabbed his coat and Claire's. He then approached Minka and wrapped her into the tightness of his arms. "You okay?" he asked low enough so that no one else heard.

Her heart squeezed at the tenderness and obvious concern. First instinct told her to deny anything could possibly be wrong and continue with the pretense.

"I'll be fine," she answered. On the contrary, she was far from fine. She had a heavy heart, a reckless mind, and after tonight, she was completely and fully exposed.

"We're family, Minka. All of us." He stretched a hand out to Claire and then the two of them ambled out of the room.

"What's going on, Minka?" Jason asked once they were alone. His scary-smart, blue eyes scanned her face for a reaction.

"I don't know," she whispered with reluctance.

"Do you want to talk about it?"

Yes. Of course, she wanted to confide in her husband and lean on him. Instead, she said, "I'm not ready."

He said nothing for a while, but his eyes pierced through her. She'd have rather he screamed or broke something and let the anger and frustration out, but instead, after a long stare, he said, "I'm going to bed." Without another glance, he left the room.

Panic set in. Her lungs constricted with every breath. She sank into the sofa and buried her face in her hands. There were holes in her tapestry, weft-threads hanging under the existing tension. She'd been crumbling more and more, losing strewn pieces of herself along the way.

Her heart twisted. The void—the black hole—in her head, deep inside her soul, slowly continued swallowing her whole and claimed its throne. No matter how she sliced and diced it, she had failed to keep her cool, to support her husband, and to have a good time.

She'd failed again. She couldn't do anything right, or ignore the feverish anxiety gnawing at her brain and weighing her down. Take tonight, for example. She should have known better, and trusted that the twins would be fine with Forrest and Claire

Another heavy sigh left her lips.

A thick, gray murk had taken a permanent spot in the space that should be filled with her love for her children, with Jason's love. She collapsed further into the sofa, into darkness.

The house was quiet. She should go to bed and make up for the many hours of lost sleep. In an hour or two, the twins would wake up. Instead, she sat motionless and drank in the silence. Unaware of the time that passed, she stared into the abyss until her anxieties leached away, and the nothingness was replaced by a need to be whole again.

The realization crawled into her consciousness. It was time to stop the cycle—seek professional help, come clean, and confess to Jason. She scrambled to her feet, and moved her aching limbs up the stairs to the bedroom she shared with Jason.

The door creaked open. She stepped in just as Jason threw his shirt on the bed, naked from the waist up—every muscle well defined, ripped to perfection, and covered with various tattoos.

Heat.

Fire.

And crazy need stirred between her thighs. No surprise there. Jason naked, half-naked, or fully dressed, always managed to produce a reaction. Lately, she just couldn't follow through.

A thick blanket of guilt smothered her heart.

They held each other's gaze for a few seconds. "I don't know where to start," she said into the silence.

"Try the beginning."

She grabbed one of the baby monitors, flicked a switch, and the screen lit up. Her attention shifted to the image of Maya sleeping peacefully on her back. "I feel..." She paused, searching for the right word. "Heavy," she whispered. Everything in her life had become difficult to lift or move.

"I can't spend the rest of my life convincing you that you're beautiful." He pulled a T-shirt from the dresser, frowned at it, and then threw it on the bed next to his shirt. "It will eventually get tiring."

Ouch. Not what she meant.

Asshole.

And yes, he could spend a lifetime convincing her she was beautiful. That was his job. They'd taken a vow—for better or worse. Marriage had no minimum time period or frequency.

"I admit that I am self-conscious about the scar tissue from the C-section. But, I wasn't talking about my weight." She pushed back the sting of his words and tried to control her flaring temper. She failed. "But thank you. I'll keep that in mind."

He frowned, his gaze drilling into her. "What scar tissue?"

How the hell had he not noticed? He touched that exact spot the first night he'd returned home from his last business trip.

Argh! Of course he'd failed to detect it. "You couldn't have noticed. Your mind is only on one thing. Sex."

"I want my wife. What's wrong with that?" He ran a hand through his blond hair. "And I'm sorry I failed to notice whatever you think is wrong with your body. Do you know why?" His eyes ate her up. It made her as uncomfortable as a chorus girl's corset and had the same effect on her breathing—constricted and shallow. "Because I don't give a fuck," Jason continued. "When I look at you, I don't search for flaws. You do such a wonderful job at that all by yourself."

The harshness of his words ran knives through her stomach. Air whooshed from her lungs. The monitor fell from her hands to the floor. Plastic snapped, and a battery rolled to her feet. Minka bowed her head. Lashes, weighed down with mascara, closed and batted away tears from spilling. Silence fell over them like a lurking monster, so thick and heavy she was sure Jason could hear the rapid beating of her heart.

Not quite sure how to respond, or react to all of this, she swallowed the painful lump clutching the back of her throat before looking at him.

Jason walked to the bed, grabbed the T-shirt, rolled it into a ball, and stuffed it back in the dresser. There was no sound in the room. Yet, they were moving.

Moving but not talking.

He walked back and forth, picking up a stray bottle and a bib. His body coiled tight with tension. Minka trudged to the bed and sat, tapping her foot up and down. She ached to crack a joke, but she knew he wouldn't laugh. Although her husband stood only a few feet away from her, he might as well be on the moon.

She longed for the intimacy that once existed between them, to touch him. Mostly, she missed her husband, lover, and everything in between—the father of her children, the love of her life and the keeper of her heart.

"Something is wrong," Jason said, breaking the cold, brittle silence sitting between them. "And you're not talking to me."

The mingled concern and frustration in his voice made her heart clench. She rose to her feet and met her husband's gaze. "I love you." Her voice dripped with desperation. He stopped pacing and pinned her with his gaze. The panic and anxiety had flown away, and yet, she still shook. Fear and shame trickled through her veins. Her head bowed. Thick curls fell forward and covered her face as her eyes aimed toward her clasped hands. "I need help, Jason."

Chapter Five

*"No space of regret can make amends for one life's
opportunity misused."*
Charles Dickens, *A Christmas Carol*

With a few, quick steps, Jason erased the space between them. "We can hire a full staff tomorrow."

The lack of help was a challenge, but the inundated feeling had very little to do with that, and everything to do with the persistent, dark clouds slugging through her mind.

Her mouth parted, ready to confide to her husband about the gray and ominous fog in her head, draining her happiness. Instead, shallow breaths fluttered through her lips.

He cupped her face and brushed her cheeks with rough-padded thumbs. "Tell me what you need from me. I'll do it." His gaze searched hers, his brows furrowed with concern.

"I'm overwhelmed," she admitted for the first time, her eyes welling with tears. "It's too much."

"I'll fix it."

That was the thing. He couldn't fix her. Not this time. She took a step back, away from his touch. "You can't fix me. I'm broken."

"We're all a little broken." A sad smile touched his lips, a reminder that he, too, was *papier-mâché*.

"I can't fit into my pre-pregnancy jeans. I want to fit into my old clothes." The pregnancy weight gain was the least of her worries, but it was so easy to use it as a blanket.

Jason exhaled. She knew where his mind was going—his mother's struggle with bulimia and the mental illness that eventually took her life.

"You gave birth to twins less than two months ago," he said in a quiet voice. "If you want, we can start working out together."

They tried that once, and it hadn't ended well. As a result, muscles she didn't know she had hurt for days. Since crawling around the house in pain was not her idea of a *sexy wife,* from then on, she had politely declined every time her husband suggested a run together, or any other form of exercise.

"I can't keep up with you."

"You can keep up." His mouth twitched into one of those sexy smiles, letting her know his mind was on another form of calorie-burning activity. Despite the fact her stomach was coiling into knots, she cracked a smile. "I want my wife back," Jason said gently, a plea in his voice.

Her heart squished in her chest. Those five little words ripped right through her. A single tear slid down her cheek, followed by another, then another.

Soon, a steady stream flowed down her face, releasing the sadness and sorrow that had been held inside her all this time.

He pulled her against his chest and enveloped her in his arms. His warm, strong embrace made her frail body feel protected. "I'm right here with you."

His voice held so much love and strength, that it broke down her barrier. No longer able to hold back, her body wracked with noisy sobs, slowly releasing her emotion with tears, and wordlessly letting Jason know of her pain.

She sagged against him, lost in his strength and maleness, her muscles becoming loose. Time passed. Jason continued to hold her and let her cry until there was nothing left. She wasn't sure how long they stood there, with her cocooned like a butterfly-to-be in his arms, until her worries slowly lost their keen sting, and optimism raised its head from the dirt.

"I think I have postpartum depression," she admitted for the first time. His grip tightened around her. "I'm ashamed to admit I need professional help." There, she'd given life to the dark emotions and spoke the big 'A' word wrapped in red and gnawing at her consciousness.

"That's not something to be ashamed of."

"I want to be the best wife, and mother to our children." She brushed a curl away from her eyes. "But I can't right now. I feel weak."

"You've been a great mother." He stroked her hair, his touch soothing the knots of tension in the pit of her stomach. "I've been traveling a lot lately. That's too much on you. It will change."

"It's not your fault."

"I can step down from my position."

"No." He loved his job. More importantly, going back to Montgomery Corporation had given him a chance to work side by side with his father, something she'd always felt had helped re-establish their once-broken father-son relationship. In addition, she had to make him understand this wasn't about anything he'd done wrong. This was about her.

"I don't feel beautiful. I have a little bit of keloid," she said, referring to the raised scar tissue where the skin had healed after her C-section.

"You're stunning." He pulled back, cupping her face once more and forcing her to look at him. "You're sexy as hell, and I love every curve, scar tissue, or whatever the hell you have." His lips brushed over her eyelids. "I am in love with you, Minka Greene Montgomery. I don't care about anything else." His lips grazed her cheeks, kissing away the streaked tears.

She sucked in a breath, tilted her head back, turned her face to him, and found his mouth with hers. Jason's tongue slid into her mouth, filling her with comfort, want, and desire. She closed her eyes and lost herself in the kiss. Their mouths molded together as their hands moved on each other, desperation in their touch. She pressed closer. The warmth of his body flowed through her, easing the anguish still stirring through her veins.

An intense need to connect physically and glue back the shattered glass took over. She slipped her hand between their bodies, unsnapping his pants. With a moan, smothered deep within his throat, he moved his mouth away from hers, no more than a fraction of an inch, such a small space that his lips still brushed hers as he spoke. "Not yet." He took hold of her hand and sat her on the bed. "First we get you—us—better. Sex can wait."

"I want to, you know," she started, needing him to understand how she loved the heady passion between them, and that her desire for him had not waned. However, there was still one huge, underlying problem. Her. "But…"

"It's okay, Minka. At least now I know what's going on. We can work through this."

"I made an appointment with Adam's therapist."

"Good. When is it?"

"Tomorrow." Until now, she'd been wrestling with whether she should go or not.

He gave her hand a gentle squeeze. "Are we going?"

"Yes. But just me, Jason. I need to do this alone. Not just for me, but for us."

"Minka…"

She turned to him, nervous but also determined, and kissed the corner of his mouth. "I can do this."

Chapter Six

"Oh, Christmas isn't just a day, it's a frame of mind and that's what's been changing. That's why I'm glad I'm here, maybe I can do something about it."
Kris Kringle—*Miracle on 34th Street*

Nine days before Christmas

Minka's hands spread like an octopus around her cup of coffee. Her fingers, numbed with cold, resisted the warmth that struggled to seep into them. The fleeting sense of confidence she had when leaving the house had flown away. Now, niggling doubts pushed away during her commute nudged her yet again.

She examined the house with the Christmas wreath hanging on the door. Under the drab, gray winter sky, it shone with an organic feel—rough, original brickwork in a rustic state. It was quaint, charming. From the outside, it looked more like a home than a shrink's office.

She should leave or best drive away. No way in hell would a few therapy sessions ease her mind. Counseling meant she had to strip those layers she'd been using to camouflage her troubled mind.

Yeah, right. She was naturally guarded, not her fault. She was born this way.

Her eyes flicked to the clock on the car dashboard, the ticking seconds told her she was right on time. Everything hinged on what she did next—hightail it out of there and catch the ferry back to the island or go inside and bare her soul to a complete stranger. She could picture her now, a little plump, smelling faintly of cigarette smoke, and smiling at her like some insipid aunt who only tolerates you because you are related.

Yep. Fun times ahead.

Minka shifted in her seat, gulped down the last of her coffee, placed the Styrofoam cup in the cup-holder, and shoved her car door open. She stood, shaky on jelly legs. A sharp December wind whipped her face, permeating the air with the smell of snow. Wise thing to do was to get back in her car and cut this trip short, no need risking the chance of being stuck in Falmouth. In the winter, the ferries were temperamental. Not reliable at all.

Excuses.

Digging her phone from her coat pocket, she glanced at the snapshot recently saved as her screen-saver. The twins, in their Christmas outfits, and Jason smiled back at her, making her feel alive, and squashing the creeping doubts.

Depression had set her inner compass spinning aimlessly. This couldn't go on any longer. It was time to point the needle north, be brave, and face this monster head-on. She had to do this. She *wanted* to do this—for the twins, Jason, and, last but not least, for her. Now or never.

Determined, she squared her shoulders and marched up the cobblestone path leading to the green front door. Her palm grazed the wood and the door flew open. In front of her stood a woman in her early thirties with sienna skin and wearing a V-neck sheath dress.

"You must be Minka Montgomery." Brown eyes instantly revealed warmth. "I'm Peyton Edwards."

Minka was sure her jaw hit the floor. Every muscle of her body froze. Adam's therapist could have leaped from the pages of *Essence* or *VOGUE*.

This was the woman she was supposed to bare her soul to?

Nope. Not gonna happen.

Lily had conveniently failed to mention that Adam's head doctor was drop-dead gorgeous. Nothing like the simpering, middle-aged woman with no dress sense, she had imagined. Nerves tingled under her skin. Instead of bolting to her car like every fiber of her being told her to do, she stood a little straighter, and shook the extended hand.

"Please, come in." Peyton stepped to the side, and Minka followed.

"When I spoke to your secretary about my appointment, I mentioned that I could only stay one-hour." Perfect. Set the expectation. Not one minute over.

"Oh, yes. She did let me know." Peyton smiled. "We only need one hour today. Let's go to my office and get started, shall we?"

"Yes. Of course."

With a slight wave, Peyton motioned ahead and started down the hall. Minka followed in silence, absorbing the cozy feel of the house. Black frames decorated the wall. She glanced at the pictures—the afternoon sun making shadows across the grass, pots of flowers, a silhouette of a woman hugging a basket of dandelions, and a closed-frame shot of a smiling child with two missing front teeth. It was simple and peaceful—evidence of the beautiful souls and the calming feel nature held.

Peyton opened a door on the left and stepped inside. Minka followed and stood awkwardly in the room. Doubt crept in and tangled into a tight nervous knot deep in her belly. Her gaze quickly swiveled around the room.

Pastel shade of green, with floor-to-ceiling windows facing acres of land, gave the room a serene and soothing atmosphere. On the white desk sat a laptop, an open notebook, a stack of papers under a turtle-shaped paperweight, and a bouquet of winter-white flowers stood in a birchwood container. The professional space appeared comfortable, projecting warmth and relaxation. Everything Minka wasn't feeling.

"This is our first visit, so there will be a lot of getting to know each other." Peyton picked up a thick, hardcover tome and the notebook from her desk, then walked to the bookshelf and scanned the titles before squeezing the volume into place. She then turned and focused her assessing eyes on Minka. "Please, sit down."

Ready to be patronized, Minka perched on the plush sofa with her hands folded primly together in her lap. Her eyes stayed on Peyton as she sat on the leather swivel chair in the middle of the room with notebook and pen in hand.

"Today's session is going to be pretty informal. We'll discuss your reason for seeking help. But first, I want to make sure you feel comfortable with me as your counselor."

Minka continued to sit motionless. At ease. Yeah right. What did she have to do to achieve that? Pull out her yoga mat, cross her legs like a Buddha, and chant 'Ohmm, Ohmm, Ohmm'?

"We'll get better results if we establish what to expect from each other. Good?"

"Um…yes."

"Honesty is the key, and in order to accomplish that, we have to achieve a level of trust, yes?"

Minka webbed her fingers together. Not that she had issues trusting others, but this was just hard. She released a deep breath, calming her nerves and removing the shutters. "Yes."

"Great. Let's talk about why you are here. What's the particular issue that led you to seek counseling?"

"Well." Minka felt Peyton's eyes on her, and her mouth went dry. She swallowed the lump lodging in the back of her throat. "I've been having a difficult time lately."

Peyton scribbled something in her notebook then focused on Minka. It unnerved her. What had she written? *This woman is crazy?*

Her heartbeat took off, thumping like a jack-hammer inside her chest.

"I understand you gave birth to twins recently."

Minka nodded. She glanced at her watch, fifty-five minutes to go.

"Congratulations. Babies are precious." Peyton smiled and her whole face lit up. "I'm sure your lives have changed quite a bit since the twins came into the picture."

Minka shrugged. "It's not so bad." *Liar. Liar. Pants on fire.* The moment they wheeled her from surgery, she'd become a mess.

"Let's talk about that—the changes in your life and the way you're feeling."

How was she supposed to explain the darkness and depression that crawled into her heart like an insidious shadow? Oh wait! Let's not forget the denial. She needed at least fifty fingers to count the many times she'd attempted to file away her anxieties and forget they ever existed.

She squeezed her hands into fists and wasn't surprised to feel her palms had moistened. *No backing out. No backing out.* "I think I have postpartum depression," she admitted in a feathery whisper.

Peyton scribbled something in her notebook. Uneasiness curled in Minka's stomach.

What was she writing over there? *War and Peace for psychos?* Mental note…head doctors needed to stop writing shit down during a session. It was a continuous stab at the patient's panic button.

"Why do you feel that way?" Peyton asked. Her attention never wavered.

Minka's fingers twitched as she ran nervous hands over her jeans, silently reminding herself she had nothing to worry about. "Most days, I struggle with these feelings."

The doctor's pen poised over her notebook as she examined Minka. "What kind of feelings?"

"I feel…" Her voice quaked as she searched for the right word. The list was rather on the long side—unaccomplished, powerless, haunted. Nervous energy spiked through her. "Unhappy." Just admitting that made her sound selfish and unappreciative. Guilt flooded her veins. This was going to be hard.

Panic crept upon her like a snake on its prey. She let out a low laugh. "I know I shouldn't feel this way. I should be happy. I have a great husband, two beautiful, healthy babies, and a wonderful circle of friends." She moved her now soaked hands to the back of her neck. Her heart felt as if her blood had become tar, struggling to keep a steady beat. "But this…melancholy mood hangs over me like a black cloud and it continues to weigh me down."

Peyton scribbled something quickly in her notebook then closed it. "Are you angry at your husband?"

"No," she answered too quickly.

"Not even a little resentful?"

Of course not. Jason was kind, loving, and sexy as sin. She was definitely the winner in the relationship. "Why would I feel that way?"

"I don't know. You tell me."

Well, lately he hadn't been around much. "I do wish he was home more." That felt good to admit. "I've often wondered if he needs to make all these trips for work. I mean, we are living in a virtual era."

"Have you talked to him about his schedule and how you feel?"

Kind of. Not really. "He offered to cut back on his travels."

"What did you say?"

"I can manage."

"So, you said no?"

The question was met by a willful silence.

"Minka, if you want your husband to be home, you should tell him."

"He should know."

"Sometimes we have to voice what we want."

Minka nodded. She knew that. One of the things she loved about her marriage was the ability to talk to Jason about anything—that is, until anxiety, the mood disorder, had become her BFF.

"I'm ashamed." She bowed her head, embarrassed of her weakness. She was the mother, the wife, the root, the springboard for her family's foundation, and yet, here she was, at a breaking point. Her eyes welled up. Struggling to keep her tears silent, she buried her face in her hands and tried to regain the slipping control. The sobs, muffled at first, as she attempted to hide her grief. Eventually, sadness took over and they gradually became louder.

Tears flowed down her face like a lone stream of water traveling in the middle of nowhere, departing from the wide river mixed of emotions—bottled-up feelings, old things lost, the changes of her body, things she was ashamed of feeling.

"Postpartum depression isn't a flaw or a weakness," Peyton said in a low, soothing voice once Minka quieted. No hint of judgment tinted her tone. "We are conditioned to believe the experience of motherhood should bring only joy and fulfillment. There's nothing wrong with admitting that being a new mom is an emotional and challenging transition." She handed Minka a box of Kleenex. "And it's okay to feel sad. You've gained something and lost something. The birth of a baby can trigger a jumble of powerful emotions—from excitement and joy, to fear and anxiety. But it can also result in something you might not expect, and that's depression."

"Sorry for crying." A hiccup shook her chest. "Sorry."

"Never apologize for being honest. Talking about your symptoms is an important step toward finding relief. Besides, that's why we're here, right?"

"Yes."

"We are here to help you get better. As I mentioned earlier, the first step of healing is to be open and honest about your feelings. Before you leave, I'm going to give you some information on a support group here in Falmouth. Some of the mothers live in Martha's Vineyard, as well. They also have a website and you can join online. But, no pressure, do it when you're ready, okay?"

"I'm ready."

Peyton gave her another one of her warm smiles that lit up her pretty face. "Remember, this is going to be a process. Think of this as more like a journey than a quick fix."

Minka swiped her hands across her face, then met Peyton's gaze. Her heart was going a mile minute, and the little voice of denial whispered, 'smile and say thanks, but no thanks.' Ready to be brave and start establishing some sort of normalcy back in her life, she took a deep breath and answered with a bit more conviction, "I'm ready."

By the time, she returned home, a serene evening had arrived and enveloped Katama in a blanket of darkness. She stood in the driveway under the fallen snow for a beat and examined the house Jason had remodeled. Her home. Feather-like flakes gently kissed her cheeks and melted. For the first time in a long time, her state of mind wasn't a blender of ice going at high speed.

She scurried across the driveway toward her house, her boots crunching through the fresh snow against the stone steps that led to her front door. As soon as she stepped inside, sharp cries echoed down the hall, throwing her once more into her worries.

The twins!

Did Jason remember to put them to sleep on their backs?

She threw her keys on the table and followed the sound to Jason's office. Her husband was nowhere in sight. Aside from being on the fussy side, and their golden-brown, wavy locks matted with what appeared to be milk, Maya and Bas seemed okay. She let out a breath. Relief.

She glanced around the room. Jason's laptop sat open, the screen displaying a list of e-mails. A half-eaten sandwich lay on a Santa Claus, red-rimmed plate atop the desk, accompanied by two empty Boston Bruins coffee mugs. The small, metal wastebasket, overflowing with crumpled paper, begged to be emptied. Someone was trying to multitask.

She walked over to the playpens, scooped the twins close to her chest, and started shushing a soothing tune into their ears. Immediately, they quieted, calmed by the body-to-body contact.

"Tired babies." She placed a kiss on each of their heads, just before a yawn escaped her mouth. Apparently, so was she. Between her first session with Peyton and the every-hour-on-the-hour feedings, she could use a recharge. Although Jason had split feeding time during the night, she'd found herself wide awake in spite of his effort. Not his fault. Her body was conditioned.

She was still rocking Maya and Bas in her arms when Jason stumbled into the room, half-drunk with sleep, and flopped into the chair in front of her. He sat, bleary-eyed and unshaven. Days-old stubble covered his jaw, his hair rumpled—not the designer kind of rumpling, either. She bit the inside of her mouth as a small smile touched her lips. Her husband had never looked sexier.

"I'll take one of those little troublemakers from you," he said, slowly rising from the chair. "Let's put them in their room for a bit so we can talk. Yes?"

"Sounds like a good idea." She handed him Maya. As she did so, she leaned into him for a quick kiss. "Give me fifteen to change their diapers and set them at ease."

"I'll help. Meet me in the family room. A hurricane named 'Bas and Maya' stormed through there."

Thirty minutes later, she entered the family room and gasped. To say a hurricane ran through the area was an understatement. Sofa pillows were strewn across the floor, along with baby clothes, Jason's tees, and the red throw. Immediate panic stirred in her stomach. She took one deep breath and silently reminding herself that a messy room was okay. It showed life.

"How do you do this every day?" Jason asked over his shoulder. He picked up the bottles, and looked at the leftover milk, seeming to contemplate whether they were salvageable.

Ummm...no. She took the bottles from him and placed them on the console table. "I managed."

Jason picked up the red blanket and threw it across the room. It landed on the couch by the window. Slowly, he sauntered to the Chesterfield coco-leather and sat. He shifted his weight, dug one hand into the corner of his seat, and pulled out two wrinkled blue onesies. After a brief examination, he rolled it into a ball and threw it in the same direction he'd thrown the blanket. Only this time, the baby clothes landed right smack on the floor by the fireplace. Well, at least it wasn't lit.

Feeling her walls closing in on her, she inhaled sharply. Peyton had suggested taking five deep breaths as a way to regain her composure. At the moment, she couldn't remember the exact words, but it was something about focusing on the simplest, shortest, and most restorative activities available to us: our breath.

Breathe in. Pause. Breathe out. Pause. Repeat five times.

"I made room for you." He patted the empty spot next to him. "How did it go?" he asked as she sat by his side.

Look at that, there was some validity to the breathing technique. It seemed to have zapped the building stress. "Well, to start, Doctor Edwards looks nothing like I'd imagined."

Jason smiled. "What did you imagine?"

Minka chuckled over her initial mental image of Peyton. "Oh, I don't know, maybe not drop-dead gorgeous."

"That bothered you?"

"Not at all. Just surprised. I guess I always pictured Edna Mode as Adam's therapist."

"The character from *The Incredibles*." It wasn't a question, but she nodded anyway, feeling a little silly as she revealed this. They'd watched the popular Disney-PIXAR movie a few times. One of her guilty pleasures she'd managed to suck Jason into watching. It was only fair since he'd gotten her to do a few things she never thought she'd do or say in her lifetime. Not that she'd been a prude, but it took a while for her to feel comfortable talking dirty, saying things like—fuck, cock, yes, I love what you're doing, don't stop.

Her face burning with embarrassment, she turned her focus to the view outside the window, where a slow majestic ballet of snowflakes continued drifting down.

Jason laughed, snapping her back to their conversation. "Peyton is an old friend of Forrest's. He was the one who suggested her to Adam."

"You know her?"

"I do through Forrest, but not the way you're thinking." He shifted his body so that they faced each other. "They went to school together. She moved to Falmouth a little over a year ago, just about the time when Adam was dealing with everything."

"She was nice."

"She is. How did it go?"

The initial assessment had been engaging, a team effort between her and Peyton. At the end of the one-hour session, she left the office feeling ready to start again and excited about moving toward the first step to healing.

"It was good," she answered. "It might run a little longer than I initially planned."

"What do we need to work on?"

"Not we." His tenderness warmed her heart. It was nice to know he'd always have her back—the same way she'd always have his. They were a team. Forever.

However, in this instance, she needed to face this hurdle alone. The one person who could make her feel better was her. "Well, mostly it needs to be me. I'm not a quick fix, more so a process. I have some deep-rooted issues I need to address."

"Such as?" he asked, his tone filled with patience.

"There are those feelings I carried for so long toward Keely and my parents."

"I thought that was over and done with?"

"I'm fine now, but I'd like to get to the root of them." She shrugged. "Who knows? Maybe they play a role in my craziness now, like my need to be a perfect mother. My mother is perfect."

"No one is perfect, and you're not crazy."

Okay, maybe crazy was too strong of a word. Perhaps just a little unhinged.

"Did you know that one day, I left the twins' bottles on the counter, and I freaked out?"

"Not a big deal. You're still breastfeeding them."

That day she hadn't been able to see that. Her emotions had been so mixed-up with thoughts of the twins demanding to be fed.

"Oh, there's the day, I left the house with my sweater backward." She let out a little chuckle thinking back on the situation. "I sat in the car and cried because I was consumed by the feeling that I'd failed." Even admitting the incident made her sound distraught. "Another time, I went shopping with the twins and realized my car keys were missing." That one topped all the others. With two babies bellowing in agony while she searched frantically for her keys, she'd almost lost it and punched a clerk.

"Why didn't you share these things with me before?"

"They didn't seem important." Peyton had advised her to communicate and discuss everything she was feeling with Jason, and to also be open to the idea of hiring full-time help, as he'd suggested. "You have a point about hiring someone. I can use the help." She pushed a wayward curl away from her face. "Any chance you can slow down on the traveling? I mean, I know it's work and—"

"Yes," Jason answered before she could finish. "I already canceled a few trips. Blake and Dad will go. I'll join virtually if I'm needed."

Minka's heart squeezed. Yeah, she had totally won the lottery when it came to her husband.

"We can start screening people together after Christmas," Jason suggested.

"I've scheduled a few more sessions with Peyton until Christmas Eve."

He nodded, seeming pleased. "We'll work around your appointments. Speaking of Christmas, we still don't have a tree." He peeked at the Rolex on his wrist. "We could drive to Herring Creek."

Christmas was only nine days away. Typically, they'd have the whole house decorated, gifts under the tree, and *A Christmas Gift for You From Phil Spector* or *A Motown Christmas* playing in the background. That is, until the twins swept through the house like a whirlwind, upending their lives. But hey, they were first time parents, a few months of insanity were allowed.

"Do they have any left?"

"I called earlier, and Marjorie said they have a few left. Do you want to drive there and pick out a tree? It may not be the prettiest."

It didn't matter. As Jason said a few days ago, it could be the Charlie Brown Christmas tree for all she cared. Celebrating Christmas meant so much more than the commercialized version of what the holiday had become. Choosing the Christmas tree was a childhood tradition both she and Jason shared and were committed to carry on with their family.

"I'd love to."

"Let's go." He rose to his feet and extended his hand to her.

"Jason." She gave him her hand. "You should probably change your shirt."

He looked at her with a puzzled frown on his forehead. "What's wrong with what I'm wearing? I like this shirt."

She did as well, especially the way the sleeves hugged his biceps. "There's dry spit up on one of your shoulders. One of the twins must have burped on you."

"I guess I should take it off then."

"You should."

With one swift movement, he stripped his shirt. Her eyes, like two iron filings lured by a magnet, instantly went to his chest. Muscles bunched and rippled. Heat seared through her and desire pooled low in her belly, catching her off guard.

"You look flushed," Jason noted. "Are you okay?"

"Um…" Her hands went to her cheeks. They were surprisingly warm. "No. I mean, yes. I'm fine." She cleared her throat. "It's a little hot in here."

His blue eyes sparkled with mischief. She was checking him out, and he'd totally caught her. So what? He was her husband. They had that 'for better or for worse, 'til death do us part' bit ingrained in their hearts. That gave her carte blanche to scope him out whenever she felt like it.

"So your rise in temperature has nothing to do with me standing here with my shirt off."

His tone was seductively playful, and Minka couldn't help smiling. Lack of self-confidence had never been part of his vocabulary. Their gazes collided and held. Beneath the cool, laid-back exterior, there was also affection shining from his eyes, and so much more. Love.

A powerful need slashed through her—a need to feel his lips, his touch, and that delirious moment when sanity ceased and their bodies exploded into bliss.

"You told me to take off my shirt, but this is not an invitation to touch, Mrs. Montgomery." Jason closed the distance between them and pressed a butterfly kiss on her lips.

Even before the kiss, her body buzzed with anticipation. Her lips parted, ready to grant him access. Just as quickly, he started pulling back, but her hands, moving of their own accord, gripped the waist of his jeans and held on like he was her lifeline.

"You're killing me," he murmured and pressed his forehead against hers before putting some distance between them. She knew what he was doing. He was giving her time to heal and make sure she wanted the physical aspect of their relationship.

"Jason."

"Minka, I can wait."

"The twins are sleeping."

"You want this?" he asked in a deep and throaty voice.

Stop or go. She knew he'd do whatever she wanted. "More than anything."

He raised a brow in a silent *You sure?*

And because he was so caring, so patient, and strong enough to help her bear whatever burden she'd face, she suddenly became very, very sure. To show him how just how much, she hooked a hand around his neck and brought his face down to hers. "I want."

"Me."

"You. Us."

Undefined emotions flickered over his features. Her heart fluttered inside her chest. Without uttering a word, he moved his right hand up to the nape of her neck and seized her mouth once again with his own. This time, the kiss changed—it was deeper and passionate with heartbreaking tenderness. And like a drug, she craved more and more.

His arms encircled her waist, drawing her tight against him, letting her feel his arousal. Her body, warm and tingly, molded to his. The kiss deepened. Their breaths mingled. Passion—dormant inside her for the last few months—exploded, came to life, and took over. Her hands groped his chest, moving maniacally down to his stomach. His muscles contracted at her touch, and she heard the soft hiss of his indrawn breath.

"Fuck."

"Yes," she pleaded between ragged breaths.

He grabbed her shoulders and held her still. Puzzled, she searched his features. He looked as tortured as she felt. "We have two crying babies." He motioned to the monitor.

Oh, right…babies, the biggest mood-killer ever. Spontaneity jumped out the window and scampered away.

"I'll get them," she said, already moving forward.

He caught her wrist. "Together, Minka. Let's do this together. We're a team."

"I know." Work in progress, she reminded herself.

"Good. Glad to hear that. Although, I must admit, they couldn't have picked a worse time to wake up."

She laughed. "We'll have to improvise."

"I thought that was improvising. Anyhow, it's probably a good thing since the snow is picking up. We should grab the tree before Marjorie closes the barn for the day."

About two hours later, they returned home. On the front door, they hung a wreath wrapped in a red bow, so that every time they came home, it was the first thing they'd see. *Christmas* by Michael Bublé played in the background as they decorated the tree.

Once done, she stepped back and inhaled. The smell of pine and snow tickled her nose. It was hard to be unmoved by that. "What do you think of the tree?"

As expected, they hadn't gotten the best one. Some of the branches were a little sparse, with holes here and there. It had flaws, like their relationship, like her. But it was beautiful, solid, and imperfectly perfect. Like them.

Jason's arm snaked around her waist, tugging her against him. "I love it."

Chapter Seven

"Christmas is all about getting your entire dysfunctional family under one roof, hoping the cops don't get called and praying that nobody gets arrested."
Anonymous

Two days until Christmas

Minka's eyes darted down the court while trying to keep up with the pace of the game—the fast breaks, the posting, the give and go, the physical fierceness and the intensity between the Wolf Pack, Tyler, and the Serrano brothers. Sweat trickled down their faces as muscles shifted and flexed under soaked T-shirts. The ball dribbled down the court, making a rhythmic thump-thump sound that was both exciting and exhausting.

Instead of being irritated or anxious, she found herself smiling and enjoying the view. Even the fact that her cell phone was back home sitting on the coffee table didn't bother her. Last week, that thought would have sent her into a near panic attack. Peyton had advised switching off for a bit would benefit her greatly, and she had to agree. For the first time in a long time, her body and mind were relaxed.

"Can they do this every three months?" Claire asked no one in particular. Her gaze fixed on the testosterone-fueled, half-court battle. "Look at them."

"It's rather beautiful to watch," Keely agreed. "It's like…art in motion."

"Puh-lease!" Lily interjected. "Three of those immature, overly-competitive egos are my brothers. There's nothing sexy about them. I'm being robbed."

"And one is your husband," Minka pointed out just as Adam scooped up the basketball. With Rafa in his face, he managed to inbound the ball to Forrest, who quickly broke for a two-on-one drive downcourt.

"Step up, or step off, Rafa?" Forrest hollered as he dribbled to the foul line.

Lily scooted forward, her eyes on Adam. "He is dreamy, isn't he? I get to do him every night. He's so lucky."

Minka's gaze followed Jason, who was guarding Max. In three counseling sessions, progress, however small, was been made. The tension had dissipated. They were laughing more, slowly reestablishing the dynamic in their strained relationship, but one major problem loomed over them. Since their last make-out session three days ago, Jason had not attempted to touch her. Her heart twisted with a twinge of concern and a touch of regret.

"Every night?" Minka asked and glanced over at her friend, sure her ears had deceived her.

"Well, not every night." Lily wrinkled her nose. "But quite a few times."

"You and Adam make Blake and I look like an old boring married couple," Keely said with a smile.

"Hey, sex between life partners is healthy," Lily responded. "It bonds them, creates joy, and relieves stress, right Minka?"

"Right," Minka whispered back. She wouldn't know about that lately. So much gained in the span of two years, yet so much that would never be the same.

"Come on, Doc." Blake called to Forrest, drawing Minka's attention back to the court. "Let's do it."

Forrest backed away and tossed a high, arching pass toward the rim. Zander jumped, hoping to tip the ball. From the left Blake flew through the air and snatched the ball. With his athleticism and vertical leap on full display, he threw down a monster two-handed dunk that shook the backboard with authority.

Blake pointed at Zander while pounding his chest. "In your face!"

"Damn, you had his balls on your chin," Jason said, grinning from ear to ear.

The Wolf Pack bumped fists. The score tied with less than five minutes left. As Max walked over, he slammed his elbow against Jason's chest with crushing force. A pang of horror shot through Minka.

Jason's shoulder jerked back as if a bullet struck it. He slowed his steps, and then shoved Max with an open palm, making him stagger back. "Watch it, ass-hole. I'm not married to your sister. I can kick your ass."

Max scoffed, clearly not affected by Jason's threat.

"Hit my friend again, and you'll say goodbye to your pretty face," Adam warned.

"Fuck off!" Maximus, the youngest of the Serrano brothers, said directly to Adam. "We still don't like you."

To emphasize Max's words, the brothers' and Tyler's arms went up. Protruding from every fist was a middle finger, which they held up for a good two seconds.

Adam blew them an air kiss as he rolled the ball over to Tyler. "Here ladies, game's tied."

Minka continued to watch from a distance. Other than the ultimate trash talking and the ball bouncing off the wooden floor, the gymnasium was dead quiet. Her thoughts drifted to the early days of their relationship, when most of their time was spent naked. Their life had been a series of natural and spontaneous adventures—a final slice of her old life now gone and replaced by planning. She rolled her shoulders and took a deep breath. Adjust, they'd have to adjust.

Tyler tossed the ball inbound to Zander, who dribbled down the court, eyes scanning for an open man. He passed it to Max, who hit a fadeaway jumper just short of the rim. Zander cut under the net and snatched the rebound, posted up, and kicked the ball back to Rafa behind the three-point line. In perfect NBA shooting guard form, Rafa released a high-arching jump shot and hollered, "Nothing but net."

Swish!

The Serrano brothers took a one-point lead.

"Take notes, pretty boys, Steph Curry in da house" Rafa said over his shoulder, already in defensive mode.

"Shouldn't you be referencing Melo? Oh wait, the Knicks suck just like your sorry asses." Jason dribbled the ball through his legs with a cocky smirk of confidence on his face. He looked quickly in her direction and threw her a slanted grin, the wickedness in his eyes sending heat coursing through her veins. Her heart picked up pace, doubling in tempo with the rhythm of the ball. A sweet ache trembled inside her with longing.

She wanted her husband but in addition to the fact that he showed no interest to go there, their house had become a revolving door of visitors—her parents, Charles, Marjorie, and Adam's and Lily's parents. Someone was always knocking on their doors—not to see them, of course, but for the babies. By the time she finally lay in Jason's arms, the touch of his skin on hers always brought her comfort, and she'd zonked out. He never woke her as he'd done in the past. Instead, he simply let her sleep.

Too bad.

Desperately needing to focus on the game instead of imagining Jason naked, she glanced at the scoreboard. With less than five seconds to go, the Wolf Pack set their offense. Rafa yelled to his teammates, "Call out the picks!" at the same moment Max ran smack into Blake's solid frame. Jason pivoted and drove hard to the hole for an easy layup. As he did so, he stepped on Max's foot, rolling his ankle. Jason gritted his teeth in obvious pain, but continued moving forward. His long arm extended toward the basket, and the ball rolled off the ends of his fingertips an inch above the rim.

Absolute silence reigned. Everything seemed to go in slow motion as the ball turned repeatedly around the edge of the circular metal, until it veered away from the net. The sound of rubber hit the polished wooden floor just as the buzzer went off, announcing end of game. All eyes turned on Peter, who was acting as referee.

"Game's over boys," Peter confirmed. "Serranos twenty-one. Locals twenty."

The Serrano brothers and Tyler gave themselves congratulatory high fives. Minka leaped to her feet and raced down the bleachers toward Jason.

"You looked winded," she said, noticing the slight limp of his steps as he walked over to shake hands with his teammates.

Jason slung one arm over her shoulder. "I'm fine."

Although he was leaning on her for support, he felt warm, solid, and wonderfully male. Swirls of desire rushed through her stomach. Instinct told her to touch, but she caught Lily smiling and giving her the thumbs up. Her lips, the ones that really didn't want to smile and give her friend the satisfaction she was looking for, crept into a grin. "Daddy's getting old," Rafa said with a smirk.

"These hackers fouled me at least three times during that drive," Jason argued.

"Whatever. I'm the referee, so I make the rules." Peter peeked at his watch. "I need to go home to my family."

In two days, they were all due back at her house for Christmas dinner. If the game today was any indication of what was to come, she might have to lock herself in her bedroom.

Zander shook his head. "There's nothing worse than pretty boys crying over losing."

Adam threw an arm over Lily's shoulder and placed a kiss on her lips. "Listen, meathead, your skinny-ass brother purposely stuck his foot out."

The Serrano brothers groaned.

Tyler snorted.

Forrest pinned Tyler with steely gray eyes. "When did you learn to ball?"

"I think I impressed your girl." Tyler grabbed a towel and wiped his face.

"You're a dead man," Forrest promised.

Rafa laughed at the threat.

"You're just mad because Claire wouldn't give you the time of day," Adam reminded his brother-in-law.

"I didn't really try. She's not my type." Rafa gloated, almost beating his chest like Tarzan.

"Umm…I'm right here children," Claire said as she pressed her small frame against Forrest. "I can hear you. And for the record, I only want this big baby."

Lily stepped away from Adam and squeezed herself between the men, hands on her hips. "Seriously, is this what I have to deal with for the rest of my life?"

All the men gave her the 'duh' look. She threw her hands up in frustration, then pinned her brothers and husband with a threatening look. "You are going to play nice. Do you hear me? All of you. It's Christmas!"

"Technically, Christmas is two days away," Rafa reminded them.

Lily let out a heavy sigh, walked up to the meanest brother of all, and pressed one finger on his chest.

"Play nice." She raised a little sister brow at him. "Or you will no longer be able to doodle your noodle. I'll personally cut off your right arm."

That drew a snicker from the crowd. Rafa took it in stride. His big arms circled around his sister. "We'll play nice. But only because you're my sister and I love you."

Something flickered inside Minka—a warm comforting feeling—hope and love. The blanket of darkness she'd been wrestling with was slowly being replaced by bursts of light. Family, she thought. Family, those acquired from friendships, and those from marriage, surrounded her. It felt good. Linking her fingers into Jason's, she whispered, "Let's go home."

"Not yet. We have to stop at Vapor. We owe these losers a few rounds. But first, you and I do this." His mouth covered hers in a sweet, heady kiss that melted her from head to toe. Her arms instantly twined around his neck and gave in to the sweet pleasure.

"Get a room!" Rafa said with disgust.

"Jesus!" Adam joined in. "Didn't you just give birth to twins?"

"Keep going like this, she'll be pregnant again in no time," Zander warned.

Minka giggled—timid at first and then bursting into full-on laughter. She wasn't sure why, but the waves kept coming. Perhaps her body just could not contain it any longer. It didn't matter. It felt good. She tried to catch her breath and snorted.

"Oops. Sorry." Wide-eyed, she pressed a hand over her lips, but Jason grabbed it away and laced their fingers together. "I love you, Jason."

He threw his arm over her shoulder once more. "I know. We need to talk."

"I know." There was so much still left unspoken between them. With a lack of intimacy, where did they go from here, and how? Tendrils of anxiety curled into her stomach. She quickly shoved it down. "We haven't had much alone time."

"The madness will fade soon."

"Is your ankle okay?"

"I'm fine. Just a sprain. Come on, time for beer." He placed a kiss on her lips. "But next time, don't point out that I look winded if front of those assholes. I'm not ready to give up my Jeep for a minivan yet."

Oh yeah, they'd talked about the possibility. "I don't think I can do it either."

"Good. We're on the same page there." His blue eyes twinkled with humor. Together, they burst out laughing. With each surge of laughter, she released some of the tension that had built between them.

Chapter Eight

*"It's not what's under the Christmas tree that
matters... it's who's around it."*
Charlie Brown—*A Charlie Brown Christmas*

Christmas Eve

A kaleidoscope of smells lingered in the house—
pine trees, cinnamon, cloves from the pumpkin
pies baking, spiced cider, and of burning wood. *Carols
of the Bells* by Pentatonix played in the background.
A smile lingered on Minka's lips as she watched her
father engulf Jason in a bear-hug. Nearby, her mother
and Charles gently rocked their grandchildren while
immersed in a conversation with Marjorie and Forrest.

Adam stood by the window talking to his in-laws.
Lily walked over with Christina cradled in her arms.
Rafa extended his arm toward his sister, who handed
her daughter over to her uncle. The attention shifted
to the adoring little girl. Smiling, Adam wrapped his
arms around Lily and placed a kiss on her shoulder.
Keely and Blake stood side by side, their bodies, as
always, barely an inch apart from each other. They
laughed over something Adam's father said.

No sign of tension. This was the meaning of Christmas—Love. Family. Enclosed on all sides by the people who mattered most. The constant poison that would fill her was nowhere in sight. Her body relaxed, and she leaned against the door, the sound of chuckling and chortling floating to her ears.

She glanced at the flickering Christmas tree. Dozens of ornaments, scattered lights—a collection of memories from Jason's and her childhood glittered amongst new traditions in the dark needles. Her gaze landed on the angel atop the tree. It wasn't fancy or at all modern, the wings on the back had once been shiny but had become dull with age, and truth be told, the face was chipped. The small crack wasn't the only thing the angel had accumulated. It was soaked in memories of Jason's childhood and drenched in happy times with his parents. The angel offered a bridge back to years past and filled a small hole left by the absence of his mother.

Minka's gaze swiveled to her husband, who was now talking to his father and Forrest. He gestured animatedly, then laughed. His eyes—crystal, clear blue—shimmered with delight. She loved his eyes, they revealed his every emotion—his need and the love that he'd bared his soul to give. A few, wayward butterflies escaped her control to bat their wings madly in the pit of her stomach.

Jason suddenly jerked his head up, looked in her direction, and held her gaze. His relaxed expression changed and became a mirror of the sharp desire that'd been consuming her the last few days.

He wanted her.

A wave of electricity buzzed through her body, sending a shiver down her spine. Jason gave her a knowing smile. He knew her all too well. She peeled herself away from the door and started heading toward him, but Keely grabbed her arm and pulled her over by the fireplace.

"How are you feeling?" Keely asked, her hazel eyes full of concern and worry. "We didn't get a chance to talk much during the game or after."

"I'm fine." Minka smiled at her twin. "Counseling is helping with normalizing my feelings." The last three meetings, they talked about her birthing experience, which hadn't been bad. But for the few days when she'd been at the hospital, she had felt very anxious, even then.

"I'm so happy to hear you sought treatment."

"I'm in a good place. I even joined a group for new mothers." To her pleasure, the experience had been refreshing. She loved her friends and family, but it was nice to be surrounded by other women struggling with the same issues as her.

"I suspected something was wrong but…" Keely shrugged. "I wasn't quite sure how to approach it."

"You could have done like Lily and forced me to admit the truth."

Keely hugged her. "Good thing we can always count on Lily to forget social niceties." The sisters broke into laughter. "Look at them." Keely motioned to where their parents were still holding the babies while talking to Adam, Blake, and Rafa. "They can't get enough of Maya and Bas. I bet if you ask them to stay for a little bit, they would."

She studied her parents with the twins. The grandparents' bond was already established. "We're in the process of hiring someone. As a matter of fact, Maxi gave us a great reference. I can't wait to meet her."

"What's her name?"

"Dee Hardy, I believe."

Keely let out a little laugh. "Oh I know who she is."

"Uh oh. Should I be concerned?"

"Nah. She's a little eccentric. You know, rich woman who fancies herself as a tree-hugger but is really a trust fund baby. In the meantime, if you need any of us, don't hesitate." Keely gave her sister's shoulder a light squeeze. "So, things are good between you and Jason?"

Minka peered at her husband the same time he looked in her direction. The stolen glances, the way he was always aware of her presence, were a few of the things she loved about him. "We're good," she answered in a whisper.

"Glad to hear that. Oh, look at that," Keely glanced toward the window, "it's starting to snow. Great party, by the way. Way to kick off our new tradition."

"Ladies, you joining us?" Blake asked.

Minka looked at her brother-in-law. Everyone stood in two parallel lines facing each other. Blake passed a few pieces of paper around. She turned to her sister. "We're playing…"

"Two-by-two," Keely finished with a grin.

"We used to play this all the time as kids with Dad and Mom." Minka's heart flipped over the childhood memory. The game was child-friendly, and one day, her own kids would be in line with everyone else.

Keely grabbed her hand. "I know. Come on, let's go have some fun."

Within seconds, she found herself standing opposite Jason. He looked at her the way all women wanted to be looked at by the man they loved. After being given a few minutes to think, at the word "Go," everyone started to act out their assigned animal—flapping their wings, stomping their hooves, waddling like a penguin—and tried to find their "mate" on the opposite side of the room.

Late in the night, Minka tiptoed down the stairs, light as a feather. She walked through the silent house, down the corridor and into the family room. She blinked. The place was black as a cave, lit only by a few fitful flames from the fireplace and the sounds of sleep from the two baby monitor displays.

Straining her eyes against the darkness, she gazed at the silhouette facing the window. Arms crossed over his chest, he stood ramrod straight, legs apart, as he stared at the clumps of wet flakes. The snow had picked up. Outside resembled a snow globe shaken by a maniac.

She crossed the room, stepped behind Jason, and wrapped her arms around his waist. The muscles cording his back contracted against her chest.

"I woke up, and you weren't next to me." She pressed a kiss on his shoulder blade.

"Waiting for the fire to die." His voice was heavy with the slightest rasp, as if he was ready to accept whatever they had become.

Her heart clenched at the thought. They'd hit a rough patch. Life had come barreling through their doors, guns blazing, but the idea of walking away from her marriage had never entered the picture. She peered at the flickering fireplace. "Party was good."

"How are you feeling?" He turned to her, their faces inches apart, leaving no room for her to hide or mask anything. "We haven't really talked much since your first session."

"We're fine," she answered, knowing although the question was directed at her, it was really about them.

After a long, searching stare, he stepped away and walked toward the fireplace. He threw a piece of wood into the glowing embers. The fire snapped and popped before hissing to life. Warmth flooded the room.

"Kids are sleeping," she said in a low voice. "I thought maybe..." She tugged her lower lip between her teeth. "We could." He stared at her, his expression unreadable. Oh, damn it, he was going to make her beg. "The thing is, Jason, we have to adjust."

"I know."

"We can't be spontaneous all the time and do it whenever, wherever."

His lips twitched into a smile. "I'm aware."

She glanced at the monitors. "And you're okay with that?"

He ran a hand over his days old stubble. "I've always been okay with the changes that come with having children. The question is, are you?"

"I'm learning how to cope."

"I'm proud of you. Once you explained everything to me, I got it."

Silence settled between them. It was neither awkward, nor comfortable.

"What now?" she asked, her voice trembled with uncertainty.

He stood, balanced and poised, as if he were expecting to choose between peace and war. "Whatever you need from me, I'll do it. For our family, for you. For us."

"I want you. I want us…really, really bad. Emotionally and physically."

"Then come to me."

Didn't she just come downstairs to find him? "I'm here."

He motioned his hands in the empty space between them. "No. You're there. I'm here. Take off the robe and come to me."

He wasn't going to make this easy. Gulp. Without a word, she untied the robe and allowed it to drop to the floor. Wearing only a camisole and her panties, she stood frozen in place feeling more naked than she'd ever felt before.

Her breasts, which were never small in the first place, were swollen and heavy from breastfeeding. The middle part around her waist was softer than before. He said nothing for a while, but she felt his eyes pierce through her. Insecurities surfaced and pushed to the forefront. Afraid that her wobbly knees might give in to the pressure, she lowered her gaze to the floor and wrapped her arms across her chest.

"You're coming?"

"I'd like to."

A grin tugged the corner of his lips. "I meant to me. I can handle everything else from there."

The heat that had been sitting in her belly spread and licked the insides of her thighs. Aroused by everything about the moment, she took a step forward. Her heart skipped a beat. She paused and glanced at Jason. Then she took another step, and another, until they stood inches apart.

"Hello, husband," she whispered.

With a gentle finger, he reoriented her face and held her gaze. His blue eyes stared straight into hers, penetrating deep into her soul. There was no smile on his lips. Only the hot intensity of his gaze gave away a glimpse of the inferno to come.

"Hello, wife. I'm in love with you, *jusqu'à la fin.*"

Until the end. Tears simmered in her eyes, and the ache in her chest—that only Jason could fulfill—intensified. "I love you." Oh, how she loved him. "I love us."

He brushed a mass of curls, which had fallen against her shoulder, to the side, dug his fingers into her scalp, and drew her head back. Then he lowered his lips to the rapid beating of her pulse, her shoulders, kissing every inch of her naked skin. Her stomach muscles quivered as tiny tremors ran through her.

"Jason…" Her breath caught on his name.

He moaned. A sense of desperation fueled his kisses and renewed her own need. A Pandora's box of emotions—lust and love twined together–swept through her with the tremendous force of a hurricane.

She lowered her lips to his shoulders and nipped. He hissed and fisted his hand in the coil of her hair, held it in a messy bundle as he fused their lips in a rough kiss. Their teeth clanged and scraped. Their tongues dueled with urgency.

Her body came alive. Her skin was hot, and her flesh damp. She wanted–she needed—Jason.

"Bedroom," she murmured against his lips.

"Here." He scooped her into his arms and carried her over to the sofa. He set her down very carefully, untangled himself from her grasp, and lowered himself onto his knees, making them eye level. "Did you pump?"

Uh oh. Where was this going? Her brows furrowed as she straightened herself. "Yes."

His hand moved to the thin strap of her camisole. "On or off?"

"On," she answered in a low voice. Not the sexiest conversation to have during sex, but this was how things were going to be for now. Their new reality, at least until she stopped breastfeeding. "And us, too. I mean we're on too."

He ran his palms over her bra, cupped her breasts and gave them a light squeeze. "We're definitely on."

Minka closed her eyes, giving in to the sensation of his hands roaming down her curves, to her hips, making her skin go up in flames. She knew what was coming and her body reacted instinctively. Her hips came off the sofa. His fingers singed a path down her legs as he slid her panties off.

She sat there helplessly, all her nerves knotted and expectant. Through hazy eyes, she watched him straighten himself, stand, and then quickly divest himself of his pants, leaving every inch of him visible. He was beautiful.

Her pulse picked up speed. The acceleration had nothing to do with fear and everything to do with what her body wanted—every inch of him in her mouth or buried deep inside her.

Nerves tingled. Sensations rushed through her body. She reached and wrapped her hand around his length.

"I won't last."

"That's okay." She slid forward and licked the tip of his rock-hard erection. "You'll owe me one," she said in a low whispery voice, then took him in her mouth in a series of slow and agonizing strokes.

A low, guttural sound escaped his throat. He muttered something in French—a word she knew was on the naughty list. He pushed himself away from her, took her hands, and dragged her down to the floor with him on top.

"First time in months," he said, voice rough. "I need to be inside you." His hands caught her hips as he settled between her and plunged every thick, long inch deep inside her.

Sparks of pleasure jolted through her. She tossed her head back, squirming under him, but not in nerves. More like she couldn't move and she wanted—needed—to touch him, to feel his mouth and hands on hers.

"So beautiful," he said, his voice laced with love and desire.

Looking into his hooded eyes, she saw that he actually meant it—always had, always would—and melted. "I wish I came to you sooner."

"Shh." He brushed a few curls off her face. "We don't want to wake up the cock-blockers."

She let out a little giggle. "They can't hear us."

He raised a brow. "Wanna bet?" Then his mouth found hers as they began to move. She arched her back, her breasts pressing against the hard planes of his chest, her hips planted against his as she met him thrust for thrust.

They moaned louder.

He thrust deeper.

They moved faster in an intoxicated dance of limbs as they became lost in time. The world narrowed to just them and this moment—on the hardwood floor with the man she had for a lifetime, their hips rocking in tandem.

"You feel so good," he whispered and bit her bottom lip.

His words and the raw desire pushed her over the edge. She forgot about the need to stay quiet and cried out. Her fingernails scraped up and down his back as pleasure shuddered through her, bursting her into a thousand pieces.

"God, I fucking love you." With a few quick pumps, he groaned and trembled over her. In her. The connection was electrifying. Perfect.

As her body floated weightlessly into space, he hugged her close until she came back to earth. Limped, she lay still, their arms and legs twined together as she listened to the comforting sounds of his beating heart.

When he moved, she held on, not ready to disconnect, and moved along with him. But he pointed for her to lie back down.

"Stay." He grabbed the red throw, joined her back on the floor, and wrapped it around them. "You hear that?"

Reeling in delight, she glanced at the clock on one of the monitors and saw midnight. Except for the thumping of their hearts, there was not a noise in the house. She drank in the silence. "It's quiet," she observed. "Merry Christmas."

"Merry Christmas." He placed a kiss on the top of her head, strong protective arms wrapped around her body. "We'll be fine." It wasn't a question but a reassurance.

In the cocoon of Jason's embrace, the rest of the world, if only for a minute, became an unimportant blur with no time, no wind, no rain. A new sense of peace washed over her. She nestled closer against him, lean and hard muscles warming her.

Happiness flowed through her blood vessels straight into her heart. "I know."

Jason was no longer just the hot stud from the bar. He was a husband, father, provider. She was no longer just Minka with her insecurities. Somewhere along the way, she had morphed into a grounded woman, still a work in progress, but more self-assured. People were depending on her—tiny babies—she was now a mother, wife, homemaker.

From newlyweds to parents, they entered new, uncharted territory. Their lives had changed. The path ahead was not clear. They would stumble for sure.

And she was okay with that. With Jason by her side through all the challenges, she wouldn't have it any other way.

She pressed a kiss to his heart, which beat heart and fast. "I love you Jason Montgomery. I love you more than you'll ever know."

"I love you Minka Montgomery. Merry Christmas to us."

The End

Mulled Apple Cider

A tasty Mulled Apple Cider which can be served with or without Rum. It's popular at our Christmas dinner and it makes the house smell fab!

- 2 quarts apple cider
- 1/2 cup brown sugar
- 1 teaspoon whole cloves
- 1 teaspoon whole allspice
- 2 cinnamon sticks
- 1/4 teaspoon salt
- 1 dash ground nutmeg
- 1 1/2 ounces rum (per mug if desired)

DIRECTIONS

With cloves and allspice in a teaball, cook all ingredients in a Crockpot on low 2-8 hours. Stir occasionally/rarely to dissolve sugar. Or cook in a pan on the stovetop on low heat 20-30 minute until it simmers.

Add 1 1/2 oz. Bacardi Gold Rum (MUST be Bacardi, accept no substitutes) per mugful when poured, if desired. Don't cook it with the Rum.

About the Author

Author Mika Jolie lives in New Jersey with her happy Chaos—her husband and their energizer bunnies. She loves to write about life experiences and matters of the heart. Let's face it, people are complicated and love can be messy. When she's not weaving life and romance into evocative tales, you can find her on a hiking adventure, apple picking, or whatever her three men can conjure up.

She loves to hear from readers. Connect with her on Facebook, Twitter, Goodreads and Amazon, or drop her an email.

Facebook: https://www.facebook.com/authormikajolie

Twitter: https://twitter.com/MikaJolie1

Goodreads: https://www.goodreads.com/author/show/8294433.Mika_Jolie

Amazon: http://amazon.com/author/mikajolie

Email: mikajolie2@gmail.com

For latest news on her current works-in-progress, interviews with fellow authors, or just to see what she's up to, check out her website: http://www.mikajolie. com or sign up for her newsletter http://mikajolie. us8.list-manage1.com/subscribe?u=031e437e36c82 d666bd5f3d46&id=af83626053 where you can hear her latest news and enjoy giveaways.

If you enjoyed reading *Wrapped in Red*, I would appreciate it if you would help others enjoy this book, too.

Recommend it. Please help others discover this book, by recommending it to friends, readers' group and discussion boards.

Review it. Please tell other readers why you like this book by reviewing it. Or visit me at http://www. mikajolie.com.

Links to My Other Books:

Martha's Way Series

The Scale – Book One

http://www.amazon.com/gp/product/ B0156VKSK4/mikajcom-20

Need You Now – Book Two

http://www.amazon.com/gp/product/ B0157C0X5M/mikajcom-20

Tattooed Hearts – Book Three

http://www.amazon.com/gp/product/ B0157E69H6/mikajcom-20

I love discovering new books. Below are two authors and their books definitely worth checking out:

Ricochet
by Allyn Lesley

What happens when your past comes back to haunt you...and seduce you?

After committing the unthinkable, the unforgivable, Tony Salvai relocates to paradise to reinvent himself and let go of the man he once was. But after one unforgettable night with a sultry and tantalizing redhead, he realizes that he can't hide from his sins—they always find a way back.

Out for vengeance, Red searches for the one man who ruined her life. She's got an agenda and a bullet with his name on it. But when she finally faces off against her sexy and remorseful enemy, will sparks fly or bullets ricochet?

Excerpt

"Who are you?"

"The new hire." She swiped the dishrag on top of the worn, brown countertop, and didn't look like she'd be offering up any more information.

If she knew me in my heyday, that'd never been her response. He raked her form up, down, then up again while he tried to decide if she were old enough to be inside a bar. Her hair was the color of a strong glass of cognac. The sides were short and neat, giving the air of a responsible adult. But the front had an 'I don't give a shit' tousled effect that made him wonder again if she was legal. The style made her oval face more interesting than it really was, but when his gaze flitted over her high cheekbones and past her feline-shaped eyes that were the color of molten pewter, he concluded she was attractive, in a strange sort of way. And he liked the way her pointy chin stuck up in the air with defiance, or maybe it was confidence.

"Are you done eye-fucking me or do you need another minute, old man?" the bartender asked. Her question was matter-of-fact, and didn't hold a lick of reprimand in it.

I like her. "The name's Tony and I'll be taking another minute."

Buy for $0.99
Amazon - http://amzn.to/1Y34YsL
iBooks - http://apple.co/1Zxxk0a
Kobo - http://bit.ly/1GUhzu4
Nook - http://bit.ly/1WCbvgR
Google Play - http://bit.ly/1HwVPPT

Cree
by LaShawn Vasser

Cree Jacobs has ever only loved one man, and for years she's worked two jobs, sometimes three to support his dreams. Her entire world centered around Cameron Jacobs. What happens when his world no longer revolves around her?

Distance has kept them apart for so long that they've become virtual strangers. Feeling lost and alone Cree realized his goals were her goals. His dreams were her dreams until tragic events forced a path of self-discovery.

Sometimes you have to stop, regroup, and find your center. Will that center lead back to love?

Excerpt

"Cameron…what's my favorite food? Outside of sewing what do I like to do for fun?"

He looked at her blankly. "Cree…"

"You couldn't possibly know because I have no idea." She touched his cheek. "I've tried to explain this to you in a way you'd understand. I need to find answers to some of those questions."

"Baby, we can do it together."

She shook her head no. "My instincts are telling me to follow you to the ends of the earth. I can't and be a whole person. I've allowed myself to be swallowed up inside your life and lost me in the process. Everything in our relationship has been about you, and I forgot about me. I came here…home to find me."

"What you're asking me to do is like cutting off half of myself."

A tear slid down her cheek. "I know. Me too, but if you're honest, we've been apart so much over the last few years that there's so much about each other we don't even know anymore. It's like our relationship stood still after high school. But you? Look at you. In all the time we've been apart, you've changed in ways that I still have to learn." She paused sadly. "And, after everything that has happened to me recently, I'm forever changed too."

"So, maybe we've changed, but, my love for you hasn't. We can figure this out."

Cree whispered, "Cameron, you've got to let me go."

Buy for $2.99
Amazon: http://amzn.to/1MJBW9t

Made in United States
North Haven, CT
04 December 2021

11935202R10055